THIS WALKER BOOK BELONGS TO:

First published 1986 by
Walker Books Ltd
87 Vauxhall Walk
London SE11 5HJ

This edition published 2001

2 4 6 8 10 9 7 5 3

© 1986 Colin West

This book has been typeset in Optima

Printed in Hong Kong

British Library Cataloguing in Publication Data:
a catalogue record for this book
is available from the British Library

ISBN 0-7445-8254-7

"Have you seen the crocodile?"

Colin West

WALKER BOOKS
AND SUBSIDIARIES
LONDON · BOSTON · SYDNEY

"Have you seen the crocodile?" asked the parrot.

"No,"
said the
dragonfly.

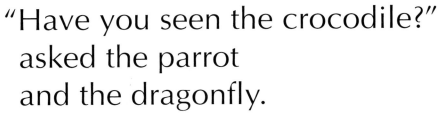

"Have you seen the crocodile?"
asked the parrot
and the dragonfly.

"No,"
said the
bumble bee.

"Have you seen the crocodile?"
asked the parrot
and the dragonfly
and the bumble bee.

"No," said the butterfly.

"Have you seen the crocodile?"
asked the parrot
and the dragonfly
and the bumble bee
and the butterfly.

"No," said the hummingbird.

"Have you seen the crocodile?"
asked the parrot
and the dragonfly
and the bumble bee
and the butterfly
and the hummingbird.

"No," said the frog.

"No one's seen the crocodile?"
    said the parrot
    and the dragonfly
    and the bumble bee
    and the butterfly
    and the hummingbird
    and the frog.

But then...

"I'VE SEEN THE CROCODILE!"
snapped the crocodile.

"Have YOU seen the parrot
and the dragonfly
and the bumble bee
and the butterfly
and the hummingbird
and the frog?"

asked the crocodile.

COLIN WEST says of the last picture in **"Have you seen the crocodile?"**, "The crocodile looks very pleased with himself, but I wonder if all the other animals escaped being gobbled up? In the previous picture, they seem to be doing a good job of escaping! By the way, did you spot the little frog hiding amongst the lily pads in the endpapers?"

Colin West enjoys working on all types of book, including poetry and story books. He is the author/illustrator of many books, including the Giggle Club titles *Buzz, Buzz, Buzz, Went Bumble-bee*; *"I Don't Care!" Said the Bear*; *One Day in the Jungle* and *"Only Joking!" Laughed the Lobster* as well as the jungle tales *"Go tell it to the toucan!"*; *"Hello, great big bullfrog!"*; *"Not me," said the monkey* and *"Pardon?" said the giraffe*. Colin lives in Epping, Essex.

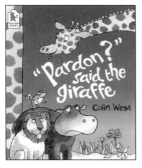

ISBN 0-7445-8257-1 (pb)

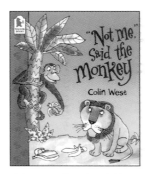

ISBN 0-7445-8256-3 (pb)

ISBN 0-7445-8255-5 (pb)

ISBN 0-7445-8253-9 (pb)